Anne of
Green Gables

Retold from the Lucy Maud Montgomery
original by Kathleen Olmstead

Illustrated by Lucy Corvino

Sterling Publishing Co., Inc.
New York

2 4 6 8 10 9 7 5 3 1

Published by Sterling Publishing Co., Inc.
387 Park Avenue South, New York, NY 10016
Copyright © 2005 by Kathleen Olmstead
Illustrations copyright © 2005 by Lucy Corvino
Distributed in Canada by Sterling Publishing
c/o Canadian Manda Group, 165 Dufferin Street
Toronto, Ontario, Canada M6K 3H6
Distributed in Great Britain and Europe by Chris Lloyd at Orca Book
Services, Stanley House, Fleets Lane, Poole BH15 3AJ, England
Distributed in Australia by Capricorn Link (Australia) Pty. Ltd.
P.O. Box 704, Windsor, NSW 2756, Australia

Printed in China
All Rights Reserved
Design by Renato Stanisic

Sterling ISBN 1-4027-2263-X

CONTENTS

CHAPTER 1

Mrs. Rachel Lynde Is Surprised

෴

One day in early June, as Mrs. Rachel Lynde looked out her window, she saw Matthew Cuthbert ride by. He was wearing a white collar and his best suit of clothes—a sure sign he was leaving Avonlea. And his horse and buggy looked newly cleaned. Where could he be going?

Mrs. Lynde knew that Matthew was a quiet man who rarely went far from home. Although she thought long and hard, she did not know what to make of what she had just seen. "I'll just step over to Green Gables and ask his sister

Marilla where he's gone and why after tea," she told herself.

Mrs. Lynde walked along the path beside the brook. This brook ran through most of Avonlea. It started near the Cuthbert place, twisted and turned, bubbled through pools and over rocks. By the time it reached the hollow near Mrs. Lynde's house, it was calm and quiet. People said that even a brook would never risk making too much noise near Mrs. Lynde's place.

Green Gables was built far back from the main road, by Marilla and Matthew's father—a man as quiet and shy as his son. It sat far back from the main road, surrounded by orchards. "No wonder Marilla and Matthew are so set in their ways, with only trees and each other to talk to," Mrs. Lynde said. "But their home certainly is lovely."

The house at Green Gables looked well cared for. There wasn't a stray stick or stone to be found in the yard. Privately, she wondered whether

Marilla Cuthbert swept that yard as often as she swept her house. One could have eaten a meal off that ground.

She knocked on the kitchen door and entered. The kitchen was large with big windows looking out on the yard and orchards. Sunlight poured in. Marilla was sitting at the table knitting.

Mrs. Lynde noticed that the table was set for three people—and that Marilla did not use her good dishes. The dinner guest must not be too important. Mrs. Lynde was now more curious than ever. Nothing unexpected ever happened at Green Gables.

"Good afternoon, Rachel," Marilla said. "How is your family?" Marilla was a tall, thin woman. Her dark hair, always twisted into a hard little knot at the back of her head, showed some gray streaks.

"We are fine. I was concerned about you, though, when I saw Matthew go by with the horse and buggy. Is everything all right?"

Marilla had expected her. She knew that Matthew would drive right past Mrs. Lynde's window, making her curious. Despite their differences—or perhaps because of them—they were friends. She tried not to smile at Rachel Lynde's attempts to discover more information.

"I am quite well today, thank you, although I had quite the headache yesterday. Matthew went to Bright River. We're getting a little boy from the orphanage in Nova Scotia. Matthew went to the train station to get him."

If Marilla had said that Matthew had gone to Bright River to fetch a kangaroo from Australia, Mrs. Lynde couldn't have been more surprised. "Is that true, Marilla? What on earth put such a notion in your head?"

Marilla spoke as if getting an orphan boy was a common, everyday event. "Matthew is getting up in years—he's sixty—his heart troubles him a great deal, and we thought a boy would be a big help. Mrs. Spencer was going to the orphanage to get herself a little girl, so we sent word asking her to bring back a boy for us. We plan to bring him up right, give him a good home, and send him to school. We got the telegram today—they'll arrive on the five-thirty train at Bright River."

"Well, Marilla," Rachel Lynde began. She prided herself on always speaking her mind, and this was no exception. "I think you are doing a foolish thing—a risky thing—bringing a stranger into your home. You know nothing of this boy or of his family."

Marilla didn't look up from her knitting. "I've had some worries myself," she admitted, "but Matthew was set on the idea. He so rarely sets his mind on anything that I felt I should give in. Besides, Rachel, there are risks with most things in life."

"Well, I hope it turns out all right," said Mrs.

Lynde. But her tone indicated she thought it unlikely.

Although she would have liked to stay and meet the orphan boy, Mrs. Lynde knew it was time to leave. She would just have time to run to the Bells' place to tell them the news before supper.

"I do feel sorry for that young boy," she said to herself. "Imagine living in that household with the Cuthberts, who know nothing of children. I often wonder if they were ever children themselves."

CHAPTER 2

Matthew Cuthbert Is Surprised

༄

It was eight miles from Avonlea to Bright River.
Matthew and his horse passed by farms and
orchards. After awhile, he began to enjoy the ride.

Matthew was tall with long gray hair that
touched his shoulders and a full brown beard.

When he reached Bright River there was no
sign of the train. Thinking he was too early, he
tied up his horse and went inside. The only person on the long platform was a girl. She was waiting for something or somebody, and, since sitting

and waiting was the only thing to do just then, she sat and waited with all her might.

Matthew asked if the five-thirty train would come soon.

"It's been in and gone half an hour ago," the stationmaster told him. "But there was someone dropped off for you—a little girl. She's sitting out there on the bench. I said she could wait inside but she said 'there was more scope for the imagination' outside. She's a strange little thing."

"Little girl?" Matthew could barely get the words out. "We're expecting a boy. Mrs. Spencer was to bring him from Nova Scotia."

"Guess there's some mistake. Mrs. Spencer left that girl here, saying you would come fetch her."

"I don't understand," said Matthew helplessly.

"Well, you better ask the girl," said the stationmaster. "I'm sure she can explain it. You'll be lucky to get a word in, though." He turned back to his work.

Poor, shy Matthew had to find a way to walk up to a girl—a strange orphan girl—and demand to know why she wasn't a boy.

She was wearing a very short, tight, ugly yellow dress. Her hair, hanging down in two thick braids, was very, very red. Her face was small, white, and thin with many, many freckles. She had been watching him with her large green eyes since he arrived.

Matthew was spared the trouble of speaking first. As soon as she realized he was looking for her, she stood up and held out her hand. "I suppose you are Matthew Cuthbert of Green Gables? I'm very glad to meet you. I was starting to worry that you'd never arrive. I decided that if I were left here I would walk down the track to that cherry tree and climb up to spend the night. It would be so lovely to wake up in white cherry blossoms, don't you think? I was sure that you would come for me by morning, though."

Matthew had taken the scrawny little hand in his. He knew he could not tell this child with the glowing eyes that there had been a mistake. He would take her home and let Marilla do that. Besides, he couldn't just leave her at the station. "I'm sorry I was late," he said shyly. "Come along. The horse is over there. Give me your bag." After a short pause, Matthew added, "Please."

"Oh, I can take it," the child said cheerfully. "I've got all my worldly goods in it, but it isn't heavy. I'm so glad you came for me—even though it would've been nice to sleep in the cherry tree. We have a long ride ahead of us, don't we? Mrs. Spencer said it was eight miles. I love driving, so I won't mind a bit. Oh, it seems so wonderful that I'm going to live with you and belong to you. I've never belonged to anybody— not really. I was in the orphanage for four months, but I'm glad that time is over. Every- one there was good and nice but they lacked imagination. As for me, I could imagine that the girl next to me was really a princess, snatched by kidnappers. I used to lie awake at night thinking of things like that because I didn't have time during the day."

Out of breath, she stopped talking when they reached the buggy. They rode in silence until they passed through an orchard of plum trees. She broke off a branch that brushed against the side of the buggy. "Isn't that beautiful? What did that white tree, leaning over the road, remind you of?" she asked.

"Well now, I dunno," said Matthew.

"Why, a bride, of course! A bride all in white with a lovely veil. I've never seen one, but I can imagine what she would look like. I've never had a pretty dress in my life, but it's all the more to look forward to, isn't it? This morning when I left the orphanage I simply imagined that I was wearing the most beautiful silk dress—I might as well imagine something worthwhile. It cheered me up right away.

"Oh, look, more cherry trees all in bloom!" She kept talking. "Prince Edward Island is so beautiful! I just love it already and am so glad I'm going to live here. But why are the roads so red? Mrs. Spencer said I must have asked her a thousand questions already, and for pity's sake not to ask any more. I suppose I had, but how are you going to find out about things if you don't ask questions?"

"Well now, I dunno," said Matthew.

"Isn't it wonderful to think of all the things there are to think about? It's such an interesting world. It wouldn't be half so interesting if we knew all about everything, would it? There'd be no scope for imagination then, would there?

"But am I talking too much? People are always telling me I do. Would you rather I didn't talk? I can stop when I make up my mind to, although it's difficult."

Matthew, much to his own surprise, was enjoying himself. Like most quiet folks, he liked people who talked a lot. They didn't expect him to keep up his end of it. But he never expected to enjoy the company of a little girl so much. "Oh, you can talk as much as you like," he said. "I don't mind."

"Oh, I'm ever so glad. I know you and I are going to get along fine. It's such a relief to talk when one wants to, and not be told not to. People laugh at me because I use big words. But if you have big ideas, you have to use big words to express them."

With one small turn, they were on the "Avenue"—a short stretch of road with trees lining both sides; a tunnel of leaves, branches, and blossoms. Its beauty struck the child dumb. She clasped her hands together and looked at the trees with awe.

When they turned onto another road she said,

"Oh, Mr. Cuthbert, that's the first place I've seen that couldn't be improved by imagination. It's so beautiful, I can feel it in my chest. It's like an ache. Have you ever had an ache like that, Mr. Cuthbert?"

"Well now, I don't think I have."

"I've felt that ache many times. I shall call that place the White Way of Delight. It really is the only name for it, you know."

They passed a gray house with a pond nearby. "Oh, look at that pond, Mr. Cuthbert. I will name it the Lake of Shining Waters."

"Well, most people call it Barry's Pond since that's Mr. Barry's house." Matthew was trying to keep up with the girl but it was hard to do.

"Does Mr. Barry have any little girls? About my age?"

"He's got one about eleven. Her name is Diana."

"Oh!" she said. "What a lovely name! And

she's *exactly* my age." The girl clapped her hands together and laughed.

"We're almost home now," Matthew said.

"Is that it over there?" She pointed to a house barely visible through the trees. "As soon as I saw it, it felt like home."

Matthew started to worry. He was glad it was Marilla who would tell this little girl there had been a mistake. How could they disappoint her? He could not bear to think of the excited light going out of her eyes.

"Listen to the trees talking in their sleep," she whispered, as he lifted her to the ground. "What nice dreams they must have!"

Then, carrying the bag with "all her worldly goods" in it, she followed him into the house.

CHAPTER 3

Marilla Cuthbert Is Surprised

❧

Marilla stopped in her tracks as Matthew and a strange little redhead walked in.

"Matthew Cuthbert, who's that?" she said. "Where's the boy?"

"There wasn't a boy," he said. "There was only her." He nodded to the child and suddenly remembered he had never asked her name.

"How could there not be a boy?" Marilla asked. "We sent word to Mrs. Spencer to bring us a boy."

"Well, she didn't. I asked the stationmaster. I

couldn't just leave her there, in any event, no matter what mistake was made."

The child remained silent, her eyes roving from one to the other. She dropped her bag. "You don't want me because I'm not a boy!" she cried. "I might have known it was all too beautiful to last. I'm going to burst into tears!"

And burst into tears she did. She buried her head in her hands and started to cry. Marilla and Matthew looked at one another. They didn't know what to do.

"Well, well, there's no need to cry," Marilla said.

"Yes, there is a need!" She lifted her head. "If you were an orphan and were told your new home isn't really yours because you aren't a boy, you would cry, too. This is

the most tragical thing that's ever happened to me!"

Something close to a smile crossed Marilla's lips—although it had been so long since she smiled it was hard to tell.

"Well, don't cry anymore. We're not going to turn you out tonight. You'll stay until we learn what happened." Marilla thought of one more thing. "And what is your name?"

"Anne Shirley," she said rather sadly. "But please call me Anne spelled with an 'e.'"

"What difference does it make?" Another rusty smile crossed Marilla's lips.

"Oh, it makes such a difference. It looks much prettier for one. Anne with an 'e' is so much more romantic, don't you think?"

"Very well, then, Anne spelled with an 'e,' can you tell me how this mistake was made? Were there no boys at the orphanage?"

"Oh, yes, many," Anne answered. "But Mrs.

Spencer said quite clearly that you wanted a girl, about eleven. So they sent me."

Anne turned to Matthew. "Oh, why didn't you tell me this at the station? If I hadn't seen the White Way of Delight and the Lake of Shining Waters, it wouldn't be so hard. It's all so tragical!"

"What on earth does she mean?" Marilla demanded. "Lake of Shining Waters?"

"She—she's talking about things we saw on our ride home. The lake is Barry's Pond," Matthew said quietly. "I should go out and tend to the mare. She'll need water." He went quickly outside.

"Let me hang up your coat, then. When Matthew comes back we'll have supper and talk about this later."

Anne couldn't eat, though—she nibbled at her food, but it was hard to swallow. "Please don't think poorly of me because I can't eat. I really wish I could. Everything is very nice."

Marilla looked at the girl. She was so tired and

sad that she could barely sit up straight. "Maybe it's time for bed," Marilla said. "Nothing can be done until morning anyway."

In a room next to the kitchen was a bed for the orphan boy—but it didn't seem right for a girl. Anne would have to sleep in the east gable room. Marilla picked up a candle and told Anne to follow her.

Anne moved slowly, taking her bag with her. She noticed that the house was very, very clean. Nothing was out of place.

"Now, get ready for bed. I'll be back to put out the candle."

Anne looked around the room. It was bare—except for a bed, a table and chair, and washstand and mirror. She put on her nightgown and jumped into bed.

Marilla came in and saw Anne's clothes scattered on the floor. She picked them up, placing them neatly on the chair.

"Good night," she said a little awkwardly.

"How can you say it's a good night? This is the worst night of my life!" Anne cried. She buried her face in the pillow.

Marilla went back to the kitchen. She did the dishes in silence as Matthew sat in the corner smoking his pipe.

"We should have gone to the orphanage ourselves," Marilla finally said. "I'll go see about this tomorrow. The girl will have to be sent back."

"Well now, Marilla, she's a nice little thing. And she's so set on staying."

Marilla was shocked. "Matthew Cuthbert! You don't mean you want to keep her?"

"We might do her some good," he said quietly. "I could hire a local boy for the chores. Anne could help you."

"I don't need any help!" said Marilla. "We wanted a boy to help you."

"Well now, Marilla, whatever you think is best."

He got up from his chair and went to bed.

Marilla was left alone with her thoughts, and there were an awful lot of them.

CHAPTER 4

Morning at Green Gables

❧

Sunlight poured through the window when Anne awoke and sat up in bed. A cherry tree was in full bloom, so close its branches brushed against the house. Anne was delighted—until she remembered she wouldn't be staying at Green Gables because she wasn't a boy!

Anne could see the Lake of Shining Waters and the house where the Barrys lived. Oh, how could she leave all of this?

Marilla stepped into the room. "Time to get dressed," she said curtly. Marilla had no idea how to speak to the child so she sounded meaner than she intended.

"Isn't it lovely?" said Anne.

"It's a big tree but it doesn't give much fruit. Always small and wormy," said Marilla.

"I don't mean just the tree, Miss Cuthbert. I mean everything is so lovely." Anne was once again close to tears. "Don't you feel as if you just love the whole world on a morning like this? And I hear the brook laughing all the way up here. I know you think it's silly since I won't be staying, but it doesn't matter. I want to remember everything!"

"You'd better get dressed and come downstairs," Marilla said. "Never mind your dreaming."

Anne dressed and was at the kitchen table in ten minutes. "I'm pretty hungry this morning, Miss Cuthbert. Mornings are lovely, don't you think? It means the day is fresh and anything is possible."

"Oh, please hold your tongue!" Marilla said as she sat down. "You talk too much, Anne Shirley." Anne did as Marilla asked and kept quiet. They ate the rest of their meal in silence.

Marilla knew that Matthew—even though he said nothing—still wanted to keep Anne. Once Matthew set his mind to something, he rarely gave in. Marilla, however, was not convinced.

"Can you wash dishes?" Marilla asked.

"Pretty well," Anne said. "But I'm better with children. I've done so much of that!"

"Fine." Marilla didn't dare ask about the children. She knew Anne would have a lot to say on the subject. "When we've finished with the morning chores we'll go ask Mrs. Spencer to clear up this mess."

Marilla kept a close eye on Anne while she washed the dishes. The girl did a fine job.

However, Marilla didn't like the way she made her bed. But she decided to say nothing.

"Why don't you go outside and play," Marilla said. "We'll leave shortly."

Anne clapped her hands with joy and raced outside.

She stopped suddenly on the porch and turned around. She came back into the kitchen with a sad face.

"I don't dare go out," said Anne. "There's no use my loving Green Gables if I can't stay here. I would just get to know and love the brook and trees and then have to leave. It would be too hard, Miss Cuthbert. I know I said just the opposite this morning—that I wanted to remember everything—but I simply can't do it. There's no use loving things if you must be torn from them, is there? If I must go back to the orphanage then I'd rather just go."

Anne looked at the windowsill where a flowerpot sat. "Miss Cuthbert? What is the name of that flower?"

"It's a tulip," said Marilla without looking up.

"Oh, I don't mean that sort of name. I mean the name you gave it. Didn't you give it a name? May I name it? I think I will call it Bonny. That's a good name for a flower, don't you think?"

"My goodness," said Marilla as she dropped her knitting into her lap. "What a silly thing, naming a plant! Who would do such a thing?"

"I like to name everything," said Anne. "It makes them seem more like people."

"I've never heard such a silly thing." Marilla went back to her knitting. She had to admit that Anne was an interesting girl. It was easy to see why Matthew wanted her to stay.

"It simply won't do," she thought to herself. "I will have to be strong."

Matthew got the horse and buggy ready. As

Marilla and Anne climbed into the seat he said, "Jerry Boot from down the road was here this morning. I told him that he could work here over the summer. So, Marilla, I'll have plenty of help."

His sister did not respond. She flicked the reins and the mare started out the gates. They moved down the road and around the bend at a quick pace.

CHAPTER 5

Anne's History

୭

"Do you know," said Anne, "I've made up my mind to enjoy this ride. I'm not going to think about going back to the orphanage but only how lovely everything is."

Anne sat up straight. "Look at those pink buds! They are perfect, don't you think? Pink is a lovely color but not for people with red hair. Have you ever known anyone with red hair as a little girl and it changed to a different color when they grew up?"

"No, I don't think I ever did," said Marilla. "I

don't think it will happen in your case either."

Anne sighed.

"Well, 'another hope is dashed.' That sounds so romantic, don't you think, Miss Cuthbert? Another hope is dashed. I read that in a book and like to say it whenever I can. Will we be passing through Avonlea? I do love the name of the town—Avonlea."

"Anne, we have five more miles to go. Why don't you tell me about yourself?"

"There isn't much to tell, I'm afraid. Both my parents died of a fever when I was still a baby. Their names were Walter and Bertha Shirley. Aren't those lovely names? I went to live with Mrs. Thomas until I was eight years old. She and her husband lived nearby and had four chil-dren—all younger than I—and I helped to take care of them. When Mr. Thomas died, his wife and kids went to live with his mother but she didn't want me. I went to live with Mrs.

Hammond since I was so good with kids. She lived up the river with her husband and eight children—including three sets of twins. Can you imagine? When Mr. Hammond died, Mrs. Hammond moved to the States and I went to the orphanage. I was there four months when Mrs. Spencer picked me out."

When Anne had finished her story, she let out a big sigh. It was tiring telling her life story.

"Were those women—Mrs. Thomas and Mrs. Hammond—good to you?" asked Marilla.

"Well," said Anne. Her face became red as she tried to think of the right words to say. "Oh, I know they meant to be as good and kind as possible. They had a lot to worry about—so many kids and so little money." She turned her face away.

"Did you ever go to school?" Marilla asked.

"Not a great deal. I went a little when I went to live with Mrs. Thomas. But with the Hammonds there was too much to do with all the twins. And, of course, I went at the orphanage. I can read pretty well, though, and say lots of poems by heart. Don't you just love poetry? Doesn't it make you feel all tingly?"

Anne turned back to happily watching everything they passed.

Marilla realized why Anne was so excited about moving to Green Gables. She had lived such a hard life. Maybe she should think about Matthew's idea. The girl talked too much, of course, but she was nice and a hard worker.

"I think," said Anne suddenly, "if I couldn't be a girl, I'd like to be a bird. It would be lovely to be a seagull, don't you think? Then I would never be far from water."

CHAPTER 6

Marilla Makes Up Her Mind

Mrs. Spencer was very surprised to see Marilla and Anne when she opened the door.

"Dear, dear," she said with a smile. "I didn't expect to see you today! How are you, Anne?"

"I'm as well as can be expected," said Anne. She walked into Mrs. Spencer's living room with a very sad face.

"I've come to see you," said Marilla, "about a strange mistake. We sent word that we wanted an eleven-year-old boy but you brought us a girl."

Mrs. Spencer was shocked. "Marilla Cuthbert,

you did no such thing! My brother Robert's girl, Nancy, brought us the message that you wanted a girl."

"We should have gone ourselves," said Marilla. "Anyhow, the mistake has been made so the only thing to do is set it right. Can we send the child back?"

"I guess so," said Mrs. Spencer. "Although Mrs. Black was just saying she wished I'd brought her a girl to help out. Perhaps she could take her? Oh, that would perfect, wouldn't it?"

When she heard this, Marilla wasn't as relieved as she thought she'd be. Did she really want to send Anne away?

Marilla thought about Mrs. Black, her bad temper, and her many children, always in trouble.

"Well, look, isn't that funny?" said Mrs. Spencer. She pointed at Mrs. Black, walking by that very moment. Mrs. Spencer called to her.

When they were all in her living room, Mrs.

Spencer told the story of the mix-up. She explained that the Cuthberts had really wanted a boy. Therefore, this little girl was in need of a home.

Mrs. Black regarded Anne from head to toe.

"Hmmm. Doesn't look like there's much to you. Are you a hard worker?"

Anne nodded.

"Well, Miss Cuthbert, I guess I can take her. If you like I can take her home right now."

Marilla looked at Anne. The sight of the little girl and her very sad face softened her heart.

"Well, I don't know," Marilla said slowly. "Matthew and I haven't decided that we wouldn't keep her. In fact, Matthew is set on letting her stay. I just wanted to find out what happened. I should talk it over with Matthew. Will that suit you, Mrs. Black?"

"I guess it will have to," she sniffed.

Anne's face started to light up. There was a flush of hope. When they were back in the buggy she said, "Oh, Miss Cuthbert, did you really say that perhaps I could stay at Green Gables?"

"Nothing is decided. I said we would think on it," said Marilla crossly. "Mrs. Black certainly needs you more than I do."

"I'd rather go back to the orphanage," said Anne.

Marilla tried not to smile.

When they arrived back at Green Gables, Matthew met them in the lane. He was very happy to see Anne still with Marilla. He helped them out of the buggy.

When Anne was upstairs, Marilla told him about their adventure and Anne's life with other families. "I've never brought up a child and I daresay I'll make a mess of it. But I'll do my best. So far as I'm concerned, Matthew, she may stay."

Matthew's shy face lit up.

"But don't you go interfering," she said to her brother. "Perhaps an old maid doesn't know much about bringing up a child but she knows more than an old man."

"There, there, Marilla, you can have your own way," said Matthew. "I'm just glad that she'll be staying. She's an interesting little thing."

"I won't tell her tonight, though," Marilla added. "She wouldn't sleep a wink. My goodness, did you ever think the day would come when Matthew and Marilla Cuthbert would adopt an orphan girl? My word!"

Marilla waited until the next afternoon to tell Anne she could stay. She watched as Anne worked very hard all morning. Marilla noticed that Anne worked quickly when she wasn't day-dreaming.

"All this dreaming will be a problem," Marilla thought.

When Anne finished her chores, she stood before Marilla, determined to learn her fate. "Oh please, Miss Cuthbert," she said. "Don't make me wait any longer. Will you be sending me away from Green Gables?"

"Matthew and I have decided to keep you—that is, if you will try to be a good little girl," Marilla responded. "Why, child, whatever is the matter?"

"I'm crying," said Anne, "but I can't think why. I'm as glad as glad can be. Oh, but this is something more than glad. To stay at Green Gables with the White Way of Delight and Lake of Shining Waters—why, it's just like heaven!"

"Anne," Marilla said rather sternly. "Please sit down and calm yourself. It won't all be fun and games, you know. You'll have to work hard and go to school."

"What am I to call you?" asked Anne. "Should I still call you Miss Cuthbert? Can I call you Aunt Marilla?"

"Heavens, no. Everyone calls me Marilla. Anything else would make me nervous."

"I'd love to call you Aunt Marilla," said Anne wistfully. "I've never had an aunt."

"No. I'm not your aunt and I don't believe in calling people names that don't belong to them."

"Do you ever imagine things different from how they are?" asked Anne.

"No."

"Oh, Miss—I mean, Marilla—you really should." Anne leaned forward in her chair. She was very excited. "I do it all the time. Just this morning I imagined I was in the picture that hangs in the hall. I was the little girl lost in the forest, needing to find my way out."

"You shouldn't spend so much time daydreaming while working," Marilla said, trying to sound cross.

Anne went back to her work, dusting the living room. Of course, she kept talking and asking questions all the while.

"Marilla?" she asked. "Do you think I will ever have a best friend in Avonlea? I've always had imaginary friends—kindred spirits—to keep me company. It entertained me while caring for the twins and working around the house. But it would be so lovely to have a *real* kindred spirit to play with."

"Diana Barry is about your age," Marilla said. "She's away visiting her family right now, though."

"Does she have red hair?" Anne stopped dusting and stood before Marilla. "It's bad enough I have red hair but it would be terrible if my best friend did, too."

Marilla rolled her eyes. "Diana has dark hair and is quite a good little girl—which is more important than being pretty."

When Anne's chores were done, she sat by the window with her elbows on the windowsill and her chin resting in her hands. She blew a couple of airy kisses past the cherry blossoms and drifted out on a sea of daydreams.

CHAPTER 7

Mrs. Rachel Lynde Is Properly Horrified

Anne had been at Green Gables for two weeks before Mrs. Lynde paid a visit. She wanted to meet Marilla's new girl.

Anne was out in the orchard when Mrs. Lynde arrived. The first thing Mrs. Lynde said to Marilla was, "I've been hearing some surprising things about you and Matthew. A girl, Marilla? And you decided to keep her?"

"And I suppose you'd like to see her," Marilla said. "I'll call her in."

Anne ran in, her face bright with excitement.

Her hair and dress were messy from playing in the trees.

"Well," said Mrs. Lynde as soon as she saw her. "They didn't pick you for your looks, did they?" Mrs. Lynde spoke her mind, as usual. "She's skinny, isn't she, Marilla? Come here, child, and let me have a closer look. My word, look at all those freckles and red hair!"

With one bound Anne stood in front of Mrs. Lynde, her face red with anger.

"How dare you call me skinny and ugly! You are a rude, mean woman and I hate you!" she cried.

"Anne!" Marilla exclaimed.

"How dare you say those things about me?" Anne continued. "You've hurt my feelings like never before. I'll never, never forgive you!"

"Anne! Go to your room this instant!" Marilla stamped her foot and pointed upstairs.

Anne burst into tears and ran out.

"Well, Marilla," Mrs. Lynde said. "I don't envy you."

"You shouldn't have picked on her about her looks," Marilla said.

"Are you defending her?" Mrs. Lynde asked.

"No." Marilla spoke carefully. "But I think you're not without fault."

"I'm surprised you're taking her side." Mrs. Lynde stood up to leave. "Quite surprised."

After Mrs. Lynde left, Marilla went to talk to Anne. How should she punish her? There was no question that Anne was rude. But was she ruder than her friend Rachel? She thought of a time when she was very young and an aunt said almost the same thing about her. Marilla recalled how much that had hurt her feelings.

Marilla walked into Anne's room to find her sitting in her chair with her arms crossed.

"You can punish me however you'd like," Anne said. "You can throw me into a deep, dark dungeon but I will never say I'm sorry."

"We're not in the habit of shutting people up in deep, dark dungeons," said Marilla, dryly. "We have so few of them in Avonlea. But I'm afraid you will have to apologize to Mrs. Lynde and that's all there is to it."

"I'll stay in my room forever, then," said Anne defiantly.

"Well, then, I'll see you in the morning," Marilla said. "Perhaps you'll feel differently. Please remember, Anne—you said you'd try to be a good girl while at Green Gables."

Anne did not come down for breakfast the next morning. Marilla told the story to Matthew. He became very angry—but at Mrs. Lynde, not Anne.

"That was a mean thing for Rachel to say," Matthew said, his face becoming red. "She had no right to say it."

"Matthew Cuthbert! Anne was rude, too,"

Marilla said. "She should learn to control her temper."

Matthew sipped his morning tea. "I suppose you're right, Marilla. But don't be too hard on her."

Marilla left the kitchen with Anne's breakfast on a tray. She also carried Anne's lunch and supper up to her room in the east gable. Anne was determined to stay in her room forever, it seemed.

That night, when Marilla was bringing the cows in from the field, Matthew slipped up the back stairs. He took a deep breath and knocked softly on Anne's bedroom door. When Anne said, "Come in," he walked quietly into her room.

"Anne," Matthew said. "How are you making out here?"

Anne was still sitting in the chair by the window, gazing out into the garden. She looked very small and unhappy.

"Pretty well, I suppose," she said. "I've been imagining quite a bit, but I feel rather lonesome."

Anne gave Matthew a small smile—although she tried for more. "But I suppose I'll have to get used to being lonely, won't I?" She went back to looking out the window.

"Think about this, Anne." Matthew sat on the side of her bed. "There's no way out of this but to say you're sorry. Both you and Mrs. Lynde said things you shouldn't have. I know her—she can stay mad a long time. I don't want you to be like that, too."

"Well," said Anne as she hung her head, "I guess I could do it for you."

"Sure." Matthew patted her shoulder. "That's just fine."

"I am sorry about it all," she said. "I was so angry yesterday but this morning I was just ashamed. I thought I could stay in my room forever to avoid the whole messy thing. But if you want me to go apologize—well, I'd do anything for you, Matthew."

"It's too lonesome downstairs without you, Anne." Matthew stood up to leave. "We're already used to you and your chatter."

"Very well," said Anne. She was already brightening up. "I'll tell Marilla right away."

"Um." Matthew paused at the door. "Maybe you shouldn't say anything about me coming upstairs."

"Wild horses won't drag the secret from me," promised Anne. "How would wild horses drag a secret from a person anyhow?" But Matthew was already gone.

A few minutes later Marilla came inside. "Marilla? May I speak to you for a moment?" was heard from upstairs.

When Marilla walked into the bedroom, Anne stood up from her chair. "I'm sorry I lost my temper and said rude things," Anne said. "And I'm willing to say so to Mrs. Lynde."

"Very well," said Marilla. "We'll go down first thing tomorrow."

Marilla walked back down to the kitchen feeling very relieved. She was worried about what to do if Anne refused for much longer. Marilla had to admit that she, too, missed the sound of Anne's voice. It was strange how quickly the house had changed since Anne arrived.

The next morning Marilla and Anne walked over to the Lyndes'.

"I'm planning what I will say," Anne said. Marilla wondered if her punishment had had any effect at all.

Mrs. Lynde was sitting on her front porch. Anne walked right up to her and dropped to one knee.

"I've come to say how very sorry I am for saying such rude things," Anne said. She clasped her hands together and bowed her head. "There are not enough words in the world to express my sorrow. Please don't look poorly on Marilla or Matthew because of my behavior. I have a terrible temper, which is not their fault. Please forgive me."

Anne clasped her hands together and bowed her head.

"There, there, get up, child," Mrs. Lynde said. "Of course, I forgive you. I guess I was a little harsh. I hope you'll forgive my words, as well."

Anne stood up quickly, her face bright and happy. "Oh, yes, Mrs. Lynde. Thank you so much!"

Anne turned to Marilla with a big smile. "This is a wonderful morning, isn't it, Marilla?" Anne didn't wait for Marilla to respond. "Mrs. Lynde? May I go play in your garden? It's so beautiful."

"Of course, child," Mrs. Lynde said. "You go right along."

When the door closed behind Anne, Rachel turned to Marilla. "She's such an odd little thing. But that's not to say she isn't enjoyable. I think you'll have quite the time raising her, Marilla."

Marilla smiled. "Yes," she thought to herself. "It certainly will be interesting living with Anne."

CHAPTER 8

At Long Last—A Kindred Spirit!

ॐ

Well, how do you like them?" said Marilla. Anne was standing beside her bed, looking at three new dresses. They were very plain—no puffy sleeves, bright colors, or frills. "I'll try to imagine that I like them," she said.

"I don't want you to imagine it," said Marilla, offended. "I can see you don't like them! What's the matter? Aren't they neat and clean?"

"Of course," said Anne, trying to be kind. "But I was hoping for something pretty to wear."

"Pretty!" Marilla huffed. "I've no time for pretty and neither should you."

"Oh, I am grateful," Anne pleaded. "It's only that I'm a little disappointed."

"Your head is too full of stories, Anne Shirley. You should pay more attention to real life. Your new dresses are just fine—plain and simple."

Anne saw that the cloth was soft and the stitches were perfectly straight and strong. "I'm sure I'll love them with time," Anne said. She gave Marilla a small smile.

Marilla sighed. "Get dressed now. We'll go to the Barrys' after breakfast when the dishes are done."

Finally Anne would meet Diana—whom she hoped would be her new best friend!

"Oh, Marilla," Anne said, "I had no idea I would be this nervous." Anne's mind was racing. What if she did something wrong? She didn't want to embarrass Marilla. And what if Diana didn't have an imagination? Or they had nothing to talk about? Anne couldn't help thinking about all the things that could go wrong.

"I've been waiting for this for so long," she said. "I'm scared that it won't be wonderful."

"Anne Shirley," Marilla said sternly. "Why don't you just wait to meet Diana and not worry so. Diana is a nice little girl. Just remember that her mother is very strict. She's not one for silliness."

Marilla's words only helped to make Anne more nervous. They walked the rest of the way in silence.

Mrs. Barry met them at her front door with a cheerful "Good morning, Marilla. And this must be Anne. How do you do?"

Anne shook Mrs. Barry's hand. "Very well, thank you," Anne said. "That's Anne with an 'e,'" she added.

Mrs. Barry smiled blankly. "Please come inside," she said.

Sitting in the kitchen was a girl Anne's age. She had long, dark hair and brown eyes. She looked almost as nervous as Anne.

"And this is my little girl," Mrs. Barry said. "Diana, come over here and meet Anne. Why don't the two of you go play in the yard?"

They waited until they were outside, among the roses and trees, before speaking.

"Oh, Diana," Anne finally said. "Do you think—oh, could we be the best of friends?"

"Why, I guess so," said Diana. "I'm glad you've come to live at Green Gables. It will be nice to have somebody to play with. No other little girls live so close."

"Will you promise," Anne said as she took Diana's hand,

"to be my best friend forever and ever? We are sure to be kindred spirits!"

Diana looked shocked. "You sure are strange," she said. "I think I'm going to like having you as my best friend," Diana laughed.

CHAPTER 9

The Delights of Anticipation

⌒

It was a lovely August morning when Anne ran into the kitchen.

"Oh, Marilla!" she cried excitedly. "You'll never guess what is going to happen."

Marilla put down the jars she was cleaning to look at Anne. "My word, what has you so worked up?"

"There's going to be a Sunday school picnic!" Anne clapped her hands and danced around the kitchen. "We're all going to the Barrys' farm. There'll be boats on the Lake of Shining Water and—can you believe it?—we're having ice cream! I've never had ice cream."

"Oh, do calm down." Marilla put her hands on her hips. "All this jumping around is giving me a headache."

Anne stopped in her tracks. "Marilla, I just remembered. I'm to bring a basket of baking but I don't know how to bake."

Marilla looked at Anne, who was suddenly so distressed by the prospect of baking. "Don't worry," Marilla said. "I'll set to baking up a nice basket for you. A Sunday school picnic is a good cause, after all."

And just as suddenly, the girl was happy again. She ran to Marilla and planted a big, wet kiss on her cheek. "Oh, thank you, thank you, thank you," she cried. "Life is so wonderful since I came to Green Gables."

It should be noted that this was the first kiss

that any child had willingly placed on Marilla's cheek. She could say nothing as Anne skipped out of the kitchen—it was hard enough trying to stop the tears.

CHAPTER 10

Anne's Confession

A few days before the picnic, Marilla came into the kitchen with a frown on her face. She found Anne shelling peas.

"Anne," she said sternly. "Have you seen my brooch?"

"Your brooch, Marilla?" Anne looked up from her work.

"Yes," she responded. "The pearl brooch that was my mother's. Have you seen it?"

Anne looked back down. "I saw it this afternoon when you were in town," said Anne, a little slowly. "I was passing your room and saw it on the cushion, so I went to look at it."

"Did you touch it?" asked Marilla.

"Y-e-s-s," admitted Anne. "I picked it up and pinned it to my shirt just to see how it would look."

"You had no right to do anything of the sort. It was very wrong. Where did you put it?"

"Oh, I put it back. I was only in your room for a minute, I promise."

"You didn't put it back," said Marilla. "The brooch is not on its cushion. It's not in my room at all!"

Anne stood up. "I did put it back! I remember it clearly. I just don't remember whether I stuck it in the pincushion or laid it on the china tray."

"I'll go and have another look," said Marilla. "If you put that brooch back, it's still there. If it isn't, I'll know you didn't, that's all!"

Marilla looked behind the dresser and under

the bed but found nothing. She was very angry. How could Anne do this—and lie about it?

Anne refused to admit that she took the brooch from the room. She insisted she put it right back.

"Fine. If that's your only answer"—Marilla stood with arms crossed—"you can go up to your room and stay there until you're ready to admit the truth."

"But the picnic?" Anne stuttered.

"You'll not go unless you confess," Marilla said sternly. "Now, upstairs!"

Anne did as she was told and slowly climbed the stairs.

When Matthew came in for afternoon tea, Marilla told him the story.

"She was admiring that brooch only last week," she said. "She even asked if I thought pearls were the souls of lilies." Marilla shook her head sadly. "I'm sure she didn't mean to lose it.

Likely she took it outside to play one of her games and lost it. It just breaks my heart, Matthew. It was Mother's brooch."

"Now, now, Marilla," Matthew said, trying to comfort her.

The day of the Sunday school picnic finally arrived. Marilla took Anne's breakfast up to her room. As soon as she opened the door, Anne began to speak.

"Very well, Marilla," she started. "I will confess to the crime. I took your brooch outside. I imagined I was a princess out for a ride on my beautiful mare. When crossing the bridge, I noticed how the brooch sparkled in the water. I leaned over to get a better look and the brooch fell into the water. I'm very sorry, Marilla—I wish I could take it all back." Anne hung her head. "And now, Marilla," Anne said, "I'd like you to punish me so that we can get it over with. I'd like to go to the picnic."

"Picnic indeed!" Marilla said. "That shall be your punishment, Anne Shirley! You won't be going to any picnic!"

"No! Oh, please, Marilla," Anne cried. "That would be too awful! It's my first chance to taste ice cream! You promised me I could go if I confessed. That's *the reason* I confessed."

"There's no reason for you to plead. You're not going and that's that."

Anne threw herself onto her bed in tears.

Marilla left the room. She spent the rest of the morning cleaning the house, trying to forget there was a weeping, upset girl upstairs. She called her down for lunch but Anne would not be moved.

After eating, Marilla went up to her own room to get her shawl that needed mending. As she took it down from its hook she noticed something sparkling. When she turned the shawl over, she saw her pearl brooch dangling from a thread.

"Oh no," Marilla gasped. "I remember now that when I took off my shawl Monday afternoon I laid it on the bureau for a minute. I suppose the brooch got caught in it somehow. Why would she tell me she took the brooch if she didn't? Oh, poor Anne! She must have made up that confession just to go to the picnic!"

She rushed to Anne's room.

"Anne," she called. "Get up, now. You haven't missed much of the picnic!"

Anne looked up with tear-filled eyes. "Pardon?"

Marilla held out the brooch. "I found this in my room. I should have believed you, Anne. I'm very sorry."

"Do you really mean that I can go?" Anne jumped up like a rocket.

"Hurry up, now," Marilla said. "I'll get your basket ready, and then you can leave."

That night, Anne returned from the picnic

tired and excited. She told Matthew and Marilla all the wonderful games they played and the children she met.

"Oh, Marilla," she said, "the ice cream was so wonderful. There was no way I could have imagined that taste!"

CHAPTER 11

A Tempest in the School Teapot

୶

Suddenly it was September and time for school. This was Anne's first chance to attend school with other children, and she was both nervous and excited.

Marilla watched her walk down the lane. Anne was such an odd girl, Marilla hoped she'd be able to get along with the other children.

When Anne returned home that night, Marilla knew she had nothing to worry about.

"I'm a little behind in my reading but it won't take me long to catch up. Math will be a bit harder, though." Anne ate the cookies Marilla had baked in honor of this special day.

"I met so many lovely girls but I, of course, still love Diana best. And Jane Andrews told me Minnie MacPherson told her she heard Prissy Andrews tell Sara Gillis I had a very pretty nose. Wasn't that lovely? Do you think it's true, Marilla? Do I have a pretty nose?"

"Your nose is nice enough," said Marilla shortly. Secretly she thought Anne's nose was pretty but she had no intention of telling her so.

"Mr. Phillips is quite strict and he pays more attention to the older children," Anne said.

"Anne," Marilla scolded. "You shouldn't speak about your teacher like that."

"Oh, I'm not saying an untruth, Marilla," Anne insisted. "You can ask anyone."

A few weeks passed and all had gone smoothly. Then one morning as they walked down the road, Diana said, "I guess Gilbert Blythe will be in school today. He's been visiting his cousins in New Brunswick all summer."

"Gilbert Blythe?" Anne remembered hearing the name at school.

"His father is the town doctor and he's ever so handsome. He's two years older than us but in our grade because he took two years off when his father was sick. They went to Alberta and Gilbert didn't go to school. He's very clever, though, Anne. You'll have a tough time beating him for Head of the Class."

"I'm glad," said Anne quickly. "I prefer the challenge. It doesn't mean as much to beat only little kids in the spelling bee."

During class, Diana leaned close to Anne. "That's Gilbert at the back of the room," she said.

He was a tall boy with curly brown hair. Anne watched as he pulled the braids of Ruby Gillis when she tried to stand up. He looked right at Anne afterward and winked.

"I think your Gilbert Blythe is handsome," confided Anne to Diana, "but very bold. It isn't polite to wink at a strange girl."

That afternoon as Anne worked hard on her math problems, Gilbert tried to get her attention. He wasn't used to having to work so hard at it. This was something new for him.

Gilbert reached across the aisle and picked up the end of Anne's long red braid. Holding it out at arm's length, he said in a whisper, "Carrots! Carrots!"

Anne heard him this time. She looked angrily back at him. "You mean boy!" she cried. "How dare you!"

And then—*Thwack!* Anne brought her slate down on Gilbert's head and cracked it—slate, not head—in two.

The Avonlea school always enjoyed a scene— and this was a good one. There were "oohs" and gasps around the room. The teacher, Mr. Phillips, stormed up to Anne. "Anne Shirley, what does this mean?" he said angrily.

Anne did not answer. It was too much to tell the whole class that Gilbert called her "carrots."

"It was my fault," Gilbert said. "I teased her."

Mr. Phillips paid no attention to Gilbert.

"It's a great disappointment to see a pupil behaving like this," Mr. Phillips said. "Anne, go and stand on the platform in front of the blackboard for the rest of the afternoon."

With a sad, white face, Anne did as she was told.

On the blackboard Mr. Phillips wrote, twice, "Ann Shirley has a very bad temper." It was a terrible punishment for Anne—one of the worst she could imagine.

When school was over, Anne marched out with her red head held high. Gilbert tried to catch her at the door.

"I'm sorry I made fun of your hair, Anne," he whispered. "Honest I am. Don't be mad at me, huh?"

Anne swept by without looking at him.

"I shall never forgive Gilbert Blythe," Anne said to Diana on their way home. "And Mr. Phillips spelled my name without an 'e,' too."

"Don't pay attention to Gilbert. He teases all the girls. He even makes fun of my hair because it's so black," Diana said. "He calls me a crow."

The next day Mr. Phillips decided to rearrange the class and put Anne next to Gilbert. She sat down and buried her face in her arms on the desk.

Gilbert took from his desk a little pink candy heart with writing on it—"You are sweet"—and slipped it under Anne's arm. Anne lifted her head, picked up the heart gingerly, and let it drop to the floor. She put her head back down and stayed that way for the rest of the afternoon.

At the end of the day, she packed up all her books, determined never to return to school again.

"But Anne," Diana cried, "you can't desert me. I'm sure Mr. Phillips will let us sit together again. And think of all the fun you'll miss if you stay home."

"If you demand it of me, Diana, then, yes, I'll stay in school," Anne said. "But I promise you—I will never speak to that Gilbert Blythe as long as I go to the Avonlea school."

Months slipped by as Anne got into her usual scrapes. Soon she was quite well known to all of Avonlea.

Diana's mother complained that Diana—quiet, good Diana—was finding trouble, with Anne's help. Mrs. Barry complained to other women that Diana was coming home with dresses dirty and torn. It seems she and Anne would play in the brook and get wet. Or they would climb trees and snag their clothes.

Anne didn't mind so much if her dresses tore—"they're so plain," she told Marilla. "But Diana's are so pretty—it's a shame when hers are ruined."

CHAPTER 12

A Concert and a Catastrophe

Marilla, can I go over to see Diana for a minute?" asked Anne, rushing down from her room.

"I don't want you running about after dark," Marilla said. "You saw Diana all day at school and you walked home together. What more do you need to say?"

"But she wants to see me," pleaded Anne. "She sent a message to me from her window with a candle. So many flashes mean a certain thing.

Diana just flashed five times, which means she needs to see me right away."

"Oh, very well, Anne," Marilla said finally. "I want you back here in ten minutes."

Anne quickly put on her coat and boots and ran down the hill to meet Diana. She was back in the kitchen just ten minutes later, breathless and excited.

"Oh, Marilla, can you believe it? Tomorrow is Diana's birthday and her mother says I can sleep overnight at their place. Diana's cousins are coming in and we're all going to a concert at the town hall." Anne could barely contain herself.

"Don't get so excited, Anne," Marilla said. "I don't think staying up late and traveling to concerts in winter is a good idea."

"But it's a very special occasion," Anne pleaded. "Couldn't we make an exception? There will be speeches and stories. Prissy Andrews is reading a poem."

"You heard what I said, Anne. Now, take off your boots and go to bed."

Once again Matthew stepped in. When Anne was safely upstairs he told Marilla that he thought Anne should go to the concert. After a short talk, Marilla walked to Anne's room to say she had changed her mind. Anne, of course, was overjoyed.

The next night's activities began with an "elegant tea" at Diana's house. Then they got dressed for their night out. Anne was a little sad because her dress was so plain next to Diana's, but not too sad. She was so excited about the evening's events that little else mattered.

Diana's cousins arrived in a sleigh. Anne and Diana joined them among the blankets and straw, marveling at the beautiful sunset as they rode. Anne paid close attention to every detail, every word spoken, because she knew this was a night to remember.

The concert was a series of thrills—all the readings and songs. The one disappointment for Anne was Gilbert Blythe's reading. Anne picked up a library book and held it in front of her face. When he was finished, and the clapping was over, she returned the book to her lap.

They returned to the Barrys' at eleven o'clock. The house was dark and quiet. Mr. Barry lit the hall lamp for them as they took off their coats and boots.

Anne suggested a race to the bedroom. They ran toward Diana's room, giggling, flung open the door, and leaped onto the bed.

And what did they find? Well, they weren't alone. As soon as they landed on the bed, they heard a muffled cry: "Merciful goodness!"

The two girls, shocked and surprised, ran just as quickly out of the room. When they were in the hall, Diana said, "Oh no. It was Aunt Josephine. She wasn't meant to arrive until tomorrow. It's so terrible, Anne, but really, have you ever heard anything so funny?" Diana giggled.

Unfortunately, Aunt Josephine didn't think it was funny. She was in a terrible mood the next morning. She had promised money for Diana's music lessons but this made her change her mind. "Why should I waste my money on such a rude girl?" she asked.

Aunt Josephine was well known for her bad temper. On her rare visits, everyone treated her with care. There was no telling what might set her off. That was the last straw for Mrs. Barry. She told Diana that she couldn't play with Anne anymore; she was a bad influence on her daughter.

"This will be our final good-bye," Diana cried. "Mother said we only have five minutes."

Anne held her best friend's hands. They both wept.

"Oh, Diana," Anne said through her tears.

"This is all my fault. I'm always getting into trouble—and I've led you astray."

"We've had so much fun!" Diana said. "You've done nothing wrong. You're the best friend—kindred spirit—that anyone could ask for. But Aunt Josephine is so angry. She can be ever so nice and generous when she wants, but has an awful temper. Mother doesn't like to cross her."

Anne hugged her best friend, holding her very tight. "Very well, Diana," she said. "We must love each other from afar."

Diana ran back toward her house. Anne watched as she disappeared behind the trees.

CHAPTER 13

Anne to the Rescue

⌒∽

The Canadian prime minister came to Prince Edward Island to give a speech. Most of Avonlea—including Marilla, Rachel Lynde, Diana's parents, and Aunt Josephine—traveled the thirty miles to hear him.

Marilla wasn't worried about leaving Anne and Matthew alone overnight. The girl was so sad and quiet lately—it was hard to lose a best friend.

Diana wasn't even allowed to speak to Anne at school. Every night Anne came home and told the Cuthberts all the things she and Diana did not do.

And so, Anne and Matthew found themselves alone by the fire one winter's night. She was struggling with her math homework.

"Matthew, did you study math in school?" she asked.

"Sure," he replied. "Don't know that I remember much, though."

"I wish you did. These are very hard. I hate to think that Gilbert will get them all right and I won't."

"Well, no," Matthew shifted in his chair. "Mr. Phillips told me last week that you were 'making rapid progress.'"

Anne and Matthew's talk was cut short by a banging on the door. Diana stood there, white-faced and breathless. She had only a shawl thrown over her shoulders.

"Diana!" Anne ran to the door. "What's the matter?"

"It's Minnie!" Diana cried. "She's so sick. She

has the croup! Mary-Jo Spencer is staying with us while Mother and Father are away, but she doesn't know what to do. Oh, Anne, Minnie is just a baby. I'm so scared."

Matthew grabbed his coat and hat and left without a word.

"He's gone for the doctor," Anne said as she got her coat. "He doesn't have to say a word. I just know."

"He'll have to go all the way to Carmody," Diana said. "Dr. Blythe went to town—and I think Dr. Blair did, too."

"There's no time to talk." Anne took Diana's hand. "I know what to do. Don't forget, I looked after three sets of twins. They always got the croup."

The two girls ran through the woods to the Barrys'.

Minnie, aged two, was truly sick. Mary-Jo paced the floor with the crying baby in her arms.

"She's pretty sick," Anne said, "but I've seen worse." Anne set to work right away.

She ordered Mary-Jo to heat some water. Diana put her sister to bed. Anne fixed up the medicine and started the long night of helping Minnie.

It was a long night and very hard work. Anne and Diana fed Minnie her medicine and kept her warm.

Matthew and the doctor finally arrived at three in the morning. Matthew had to go all the way to Carmody to find him, and the trip was a long one.

The doctor examined Minnie. He said that the danger had passed. "You've done a fine job, Miss Shirley," he said.

"I was very worried for a while there," Anne admitted. "Although I said nothing to Diana or Mary-Jo."

Matthew and Anne walked back to Green

Gables in the bright moonlight. Even though she was very tired, she couldn't stop talking. "I used to complain about taking care of so many twins," she said, "but I'm glad of it, now. I knew what to do and could keep calm. It wouldn't have helped if I were crying, too."

"You did a fine thing, Anne-girl," Matthew said. "You should head up to bed and get some sleep. Don't worry about school tomorrow—I'll do your chores."

"I hate to miss school and fall behind Gil—I mean, the other kids," Anne said sleepily. "I just don't think I could get up no matter how hard I tried."

In fact, Anne didn't wake up until lunchtime. She walked into the bright kitchen to find Marilla cooking.

"Well, now, if it isn't little Dr. Shirley." Marilla smiled.

"Marilla," said Anne happily. "How was your trip? Did you see the prime minister?"

"I did—and the trip was fine. Matthew told me about your night." Marilla put her hands on Anne's shoulders. "It's a good thing you were here. I wouldn't have been much help—I've never seen a child with the croup.

"You should know," Marilla added, "Mrs. Barry was here this morning. The doctor told her that you saved little Minnie's life. He never would have gotten there in time."

"I'm so glad," Anne said. She felt like she might cry from happiness and relief.

"She also said you could come back and play with Diana anytime."

"Really, Marilla?" Anne clapped her hands. "Oh, could that be true?"

"Why don't you run down there to see for yourself?"

Anne dressed quickly and ran out the door. She and Diana could be chums again. The next day at school, they asked Mr. Phillips to seat them together again. Of course, he couldn't refuse.

$\sim$

There was one more thing to take care of. Anne wanted to apologize to Aunt Josephine, too. She marched into the Barrys' living room where the older woman sat.

"Who are you?" demanded Miss Josephine Barry.

"I'm Anne of Green Gables," she said, "and I've come to confess."

"Confess what?"

"The race—and jumping onto the bed—that was my idea. Diana would never do such a thing on her own." Anne held her hands behind her back, trying to stop them from shaking.

"I think Diana did her share," Miss Barry said stiffly. But she wasn't angry anymore—not since Anne saved little Minnie. Still, she wanted to see what Anne would say.

"It was all in fun," Anne said. "Diana is looking forward to her music lessons. Please don't stop her from taking them because of something I did. I can be very silly sometimes—everyone knows that—but I would never do anything to hurt Diana."

"I don't know if I agree with your idea of fun." Miss Barry tried not to smile. "That was not the kind of thing we did as little girls. It was quite the shock to have two little girls pounce on me while sound asleep. You've no idea."

"No," Anne said, "but I can imagine. Have you an imagination, Miss Barry? If so, put yourself in our place. It was Diana's birthday, and I had never experienced anything so wonderful as a night-time concert. You might be used to sleeping in spare beds, but for me, an orphan girl, I'd never had such an honor before."

This time, Miss Barry laughed out loud. Diana, listening from the hall, sighed with relief.

"I'm afraid my imagination is a little rusty— it's so long since I used it," she said. "I daresay you've made a strong case. Now, come sit and tell me about yourself."

"I'm sorry, but I can't," Anne replied. "I'd like to, but I must go home to Green Gables. Marilla has been very kind to take me in and I don't want to cause her any worry."

"Very well, then," Miss Barry said. "Promise me you'll stop by for a talk now and then."

When Anne got home, she told Marilla about their little talk.

"It's funny, Marilla," Anne said while washing the dishes. "It seems Miss Barry was a kindred spirit after all. I guess they're not as scarce as I thought. It's splendid to find out how many there are!"

At the end of the school year, Mr. Phillips announced he wouldn't be returning in the fall. All the girls cried—including Anne.

"Anne Shirley," said Marilla. "You always said Mr. Phillips wasn't a good teacher—and look at you now—all red-eyed and weepy."

"I know, Marilla," she replied. "I tried not to cry—honest I did—but his farewell speech was so sweet and lovely, I just couldn't help myself."

This was the start of a very busy summer for Anne. Thankfully, it passed without too much trouble.

Oh, there were the little things that Anne did. When lost in dreaming, she walked clean over the edge of the log bridge into the brook. Marilla had grown used to Anne, and her strange ways didn't bother her.

One morning Anne said, "Marilla, isn't it nice to think that tomorrow is a new day with no mistakes in it yet?"

"I'll bet you'll make plenty, though," said Marilla. "I never saw anyone so ready to make mistakes, Anne."

"Yes, and don't I know it," admitted Anne. "But have you ever noticed one encouraging thing about me, Marilla? I never make the same mistake twice."

CHAPTER 14

Miss Stacy and Her Pupils
Put On a Concert

∽

The new school year started with much excitement. As soon as Anne met Miss Stacy, she knew her new teacher would be wonderful.

"You would love her voice, Marilla," Anne said. As always, she told every single detail about her day. "When she reads poems out loud it's perfectly lovely!"

Marilla continued with her work, rolling out piecrusts. She was used to hearing Anne's constant chatter.

Anne enjoyed her studies a great deal—even

math didn't seem so awful. She still had to devote more time to it than other subjects. But she finally could make sense of it. She felt like all her hard work was paying off.

"Miss Stacy said we'll be putting on a play this year. And would you believe it, Marilla? I'm to play the Fairy Queen! The whole class clapped when she told us. I'm ever so nervous and excited. I've already learned some of my lines—even though it's not until Christmastime."

Poor Matthew! Having Anne in a play meant Green Gables was often filled with excited, giggling girls. He was so shy that he could barely say "hello." One day, while watching them put on their coats, he noticed something strange. All the girls wore pretty, frilly dresses with puffed sleeves. All except Anne. Her dress was plain with straight lines and an apron. For the first time, Matthew noticed that Anne was dressed the same as Marilla.

Matthew was determined to get Anne a dress with puffed sleeves. The very next day, he went to the store in Avonlea to buy one. But he didn't have the nerve to talk to the salesgirl.

So Matthew went to Mrs. Lynde's to see if she could make Anne a dress. "I'd like it to be a surprise, if you don't mind," he said. "For Anne and Marilla."

"Don't you worry about a thing," Mrs. Lynde said. "I think it's time that girl had something new to wear. Marilla dresses her like an old lady."

Matthew surprised Anne with her new dress on Christmas morning. The night before, Marilla learned of the present and wasn't too pleased. "She shouldn't be thinking about silly things like pretty dresses," Marilla said.

Matthew didn't expect Anne's reaction, though. When she burst into tears, he thought he must have done something wrong. "Do-do you n-not like them, Anne?" Matthew stuttered.

"Oh, Matthew." Anne could barely get the words out. She draped the dress over the back of a chair. It was dark brown with a matching silk headband.

She stared at it with her hands clasped in front of her. "It's the most beautiful, most wonderful, most perfect dress I have ever seen!"

Anne threw her arms around Matthew's neck and kissed his cheek. "And puffed sleeves, Matthew! It's everything I dreamed it would be."

Matthew blushed more than ever. "Well now, Anne," he said. "That's just grand."

Marilla watched from the side. She was surprised to realize she was quite happy about it. She could even feel her eyes well up a bit. Marilla quickly announced they should sit down for breakfast and stop this silliness. She was in the kitchen before they could notice her wiping her eyes.

On the night of the Avonlea school play,

Anne wore her new brown dress. She stood on stage and read her lines with confidence.

"Did you see Gilbert?" Diana asked afterward.

"Diana," Anne said haughtily, "you know that I have no time for that boy."

"But Anne," Diana said, "as you left the stage, a flower fell from your bouquet. I saw Gilbert—with my own eyes—pick it up and put it in his pocket. Isn't that lovely?"

"It's of no concern of mine what he does," Anne replied. "Please don't even bother to mention his name to me. I simply don't care."

Diana looked at her best friend and thought perhaps there was a bit more to this story.

ᴄ⌀

It was hard to settle down after the excitement of the school play. Anne decided that they should form a story club.

"We simply can't go back to life before the concert," Anne told Diana. "Let's you and I have a story club."

At first, there was only Anne and Diana, but soon Ruby Gillis and Jane Andrews joined. That is how it all started. They met as often as they could and read their stories out loud. Their stories were about heroes on horses, women writers finding true love, and people being saved from danger. Anne's stories often had tragic endings. She thought that was more romantic. "All the best novels have sad endings," she said.

The girls talked about more than stories, of course. Miss Stacy and school were popular topics. And how they were all growing up so fast.

"It won't be long before we'll be able to put our hair up," said Diana.

"I'm not in a hurry," Anne replied. "I'm happy being a girl."

Ruby Gillis liked to talk about boys—Gilbert Blythe in particular. "He's ever so handsome. Even you must think so, Anne."

Anne turned her face away. "Gilbert?" she sniffed. "I barely notice that he's there."

CHAPTER 15

Vanity Gets the Best of Anne

ᘓ

One April night, as Marilla walked home, she noticed that spring had finally arrived. Flowers were starting to bloom, waking up after a long winter's sleep. Marilla felt happy without knowing why.

She could see Green Gables through the trees. It looked so beautiful with the setting sun reflected in the windows. "It will be nice to sit beside the warm fire," Marilla thought. She had asked Anne to have the tea ready for five o'clock. Life at Green Gables was so different since Anne arrived, Marilla thought as she smiled to herself.

When she entered the kitchen she found no fire and no tea. She was both disappointed and irritated. "Where is that girl?" she muttered as she took off her second-best dress to prepare supper.

Matthew came in from plowing and was waiting for his tea. He watched Marilla stamp about the kitchen, banging pots and complaining about Anne. "She's off somewhere with Diana, forgetting all about her chores. Her head is full of nonsense and you just never know what she'll do next. She had no right to leave the house when there was work to do. I must say, it surprises me—it's not like Anne to be so disobedient."

"Well, I dunno," said Matthew, sitting patiently in his corner. "Maybe she has a good reason."

"Matthew Cuthbert, I knew you would take her side!"

Suppertime came and went with no sign of

Anne. Marilla expected her to run through the door, breathless and full of apologies. But the house was quiet and dark. Marilla went to look for a candle in Anne's room. Lighting it, she turned around to see Anne herself lying on the bed, face-down in the pillows.

"Goodness me," said Marilla. "Have you been asleep?"

"No," came the muffled reply.

"Are you feeling sick?" Marilla asked. She went to feel Anne's forehead.

Anne moved her head away. "Oh please, Marilla, go away and don't look at me! I am in the depths of despair! My life is absolutely ruined. It's over!"

"Anne Shirley, whatever is the matter with you? Get up right this minute and tell me." Marilla pulled back the covers from Anne's bed. She held the candle up to get a better look as Anne slowly pulled herself up.

"Look at my hair, Marilla," she whispered.

"My goodness," Marilla gasped. "What have you done? Your hair is green!"

It wasn't an ordinary green, like the color of grass or trees. It was a dull brownish green with streaks of the original red. Marilla thought she had never seen a color so ugly in all her life.

"Yes, it's green," moaned Anne. "I thought nothing could be as bad as red hair. I now know it's ten times worse to have green hair. Oh, Marilla, I feel so awful!"

"I knew life was too quiet in this house. It's been months since your last scrape." Marilla stood tall beside Anne. "All right now, what happened?"

"I dyed it." Anne began to cry again. "He told me it would turn my hair a beautiful raven black. Miss Stacy says we should trust people unless they've given us cause not to, and I had no reason not to. But Marilla, my hair isn't a beautiful raven black, is it? It's a hideous, horrible green!"

Marilla took her by the shoulders. "Who are you talking about, Anne?"

"I bought the dye at the general store when Matthew and I were in Carmody. The clerk said he'd reduce the price for me, as I only had fifty cents and it cost seventy-five. I followed all the directions, and used the whole bottle, but when I saw what color my hair was—oh, Marilla, whatever will I do?"

"I'm glad you can see what your foolishness has brought you, Anne." Marilla patted her gently on the back. "You really must think things through more carefully."

She set about washing Anne's hair. She tried several times but the color didn't change. Poor Anne exclaimed, "I will never live this down! I am the unhappiest girl in Prince Edward Island!"

Anne was inconsolable. She stayed home from school and washed her hair every day. Only

Diana knew her secret, but kept her word and told no one. Finally, Marilla decided that the only solution was to cut her hair. This made Anne very sad. But she knew Marilla was right.

"Please cut it off at once, Marilla. Oh, I feel that my heart is broken. This is such an unromantic affliction. Girls in books lose their hair in fevers or sell it to get money for some good deed. There is nothing comforting in having your hair cut off because you've dyed it a dreadful color. I'm going to weep all the time you're cutting it off, if it won't interfere."

Marilla had to cut her hair very, very short to remove all the offending color. Anne looked in the mirror with calm despair. "I will look in this mirror every day to remind myself how silly I am. I won't even try to imagine it away.

Even though I hated that red hair, it *was* nice and thick and curly."

Anne's clipped head made a sensation in school the following Monday, but to her relief nobody guessed the real reason for it.

Later that night, Anne told Marilla, who was lying on the couch with one of her headaches, "Diana says when my hair begins to grow I can tie a black velvet ribbon around my head with a bow on one side. She thinks it will be very becoming. I will call it a snood—that sounds so romantic. But am I talking too much, Marilla? Does your head hurt?"

"I'm feeling much better now, thank you. As for your chatter, I don't know that I mind it—I've gotten so used to it."

Which was Marilla's way of saying that she liked to hear it.

CHAPTER 16

An Unfortunate Lily Maid

∽

O f course, Anne, you must be Elaine," Diana
said.

"Yes," said Jane. "I could never keep still."

Ruby only shook her head to say she could
never imagine floating down the river in a boat
all by herself.

"I think it's silly to have a redheaded Elaine,"
Anne said. "Elaine should have long blond hair.
But if I'm the only one willing, it'll have to do."

"Oh, it's turning a lovely auburn," said Diana,
about Anne's hair. She admired the short, curly

locks with the black hair ribbon. It had been more than a year since Anne's green-hair days.

"You are very kind, Diana. I couldn't ask for a better friend."

It was Anne's idea to act out a poem they had read in class. It was about Elaine, the lily maid, who lived in the time of Camelot and the Knights of the Round Table. Anne loved stories about King Arthur and his brave knights. They were such romantic and exciting stories. Anne longed to go back to the times of Camelot, with King Arthur and the Knights of the Round Table, because those times were so romantic.

The other three girls held the boat steady while Anne stepped in. She lay down, resting her head on a pillow. Anne crossed her arms over her chest and closed her eyes.

"Oh, she really does look dead," Ruby mused.

"Don't spoil the effect, Ruby," Anne scolded with eyes still closed. "Jane, you should lead the ceremony. It's not right for Elaine to speak when she should be dead."

Jane did as she was told and said the proper lines for a good-bye. The girls then pushed the boat downstream.

The girls rushed along the bank. They were to meet the boat again around the bend.

Anne's trip took a new turn, though, when the boat began to leak. She didn't notice until it was too late. She scrambled to her feet, grabbed her pillow, and looked for the oars. The oars were still on the dock! When she realized how much trouble she was in, Anne let out a little scream.

An old tree stump was leaning out from the bank. Anne had the good sense to grab hold of it and pull herself up. Then her dress became tangled on the branches and she was trapped.

She sat there not knowing what to do. Where were her friends? Why didn't they come looking for her?

Then, just as she thought she could wait no longer, she saw Gilbert Blythe rowing toward her.

He looked up and almost jumped from fright when he saw Anne hanging above him.

"Anne Shirley! What are you doing up there?" he exclaimed.

He pulled close and held out his hand. There was nothing else for Anne to do but take it and climb into his boat.

"How did you get up there?" Gilbert asked. He was both amused and confused. Life was never simple when Anne Shirley was around.

"We were playing 'Elaine,'" Anne explained. "I was floating downriver to Camelot when the boat sprang a leak. The girls must have run for help. Could you please drop me off at the landing?"

She jumped ashore—refusing Gilbert's outstretched hand—and started walking away. "Thank you very much," she called over her shoulder.

"Anne," Gilbert called. "Wait. Can't we be friends? I'm sorry I called you 'carrots' that day, but it was so long ago. I think your hair is very pretty now—honest I do. Let's be friends."

Gilbert's voice sounded half shy, half eager. Anne's heart gave a quick, queer little beat. She almost said "yes," but remembered how angry she had been all those years ago. He had made fun of her hair and she could never forgive him.

"No," she said coldly, "I shall never be friends with you, Gilbert Blythe!"

"Fine," he said angrily. "I will never ask you again. Good-bye!" He pushed his boat from the bank. Gilbert rowed away without looking back.

She felt an odd sensation. Was it regret? Should she have answered him differently? She felt like crying—like she had just lost something very special.

Anne walked up the path feeling sad. She met

Diana, Jane, and Ruby along the way. They were in quite a state.

"Oh, Anne!" Diana cried. "We thought we'd lost you forever!" She threw her arms around her best friend.

They explained that when they saw the boat quickly filling up with water, coming around the bend without Anne, they thought surely she had drowned.

Anne told them how she climbed onto a tree and was rescued by Gilbert.

"Why, it's so romantic," said Diana. "Elaine was saved by a knight."

"Does this mean you'll speak to Gil from now on?" Ruby asked.

"Of course I won't." Anne tried to regain some of her old spirit. "I'm sorry that I frightened you girls. It's all my fault. I'm feeling very unlucky today."

When Marilla heard of Anne's adventure she

was very angry. "When will you ever learn?" she exclaimed.

"I've learned a good lesson today," Anne said sadly. "I've learned that Avonlea is not the place for romance."

"Well," said Marilla, "that's the first sensible thing you've said."

Matthew, who was sitting quietly in his corner, laid a hand on Anne's shoulder after Marilla had gone out.

"Don't give up on all your romance, Anne," he whispered shyly. "A little of it is a good thing— not too much, of course—but keep a little of it, Anne, keep a little of it."

CHAPTER 17

An Epoch in Anne's Life

〜

One night as Anne was bringing in the cows from the field, Diana told Anne the most wonderful news.

"You will never guess," Diana laughed. "Aunt Josephine has invited us to visit her in the city and see the fair. Can you believe it?"

"It seems too wonderful," Anne squealed. "What if Marilla won't let me go? You know how she feels about concerts and the like."

"We'll have my mother ask her," Diana said. "That's sure to help."

And help it did. Marilla agreed to let Anne go.

They got up bright and early for the thirty-mile ride to Charlottetown. Miss Barry met them at the door with a big hug.

It was such a magical time. Anne and Diana saw all kinds of animals and crafts at the fair. They ate fresh-baked pie and watched as people from Avonlea won prizes, so there was plenty to cheer about. The high point for Anne was watching a man go up in a hot-air balloon. Another night, Miss Barry took them out for ice cream.

It all seemed like heaven to Anne, but she was happy to return home to Avonlea and Green Gables. "I don't think I'm cut out for city life," she told Marilla. "I felt lonesome without you and Matthew—not to mention the orchard and the Lake of Shining Waters."

"I hope you thanked Miss Barry for her kindness," Marilla said.

"Oh yes, I did. And she thanked us both for

the visit, too. Miss Barry said she first thought you were an old fool for keeping an orphan girl. But now she's changed her mind. She said I was lovely to have around the house."

"You shouldn't brag, Anne," Marilla scolded.

"I'm not bragging, Marilla. That's exactly what she said."

"Well, then, I guess I agree with Miss Barry. And I'm awful glad to have you home."

CHAPTER 18

The Queen's Class Is Organized

◠

One night as they sat before the fire, Marilla brought up an important subject. "Anne," she said. "Miss Stacy was here to talk about you."

Anne sat up with fright. She tried to remember if she had done anything awful lately but nothing came to mind. Even her adventure as Elaine was long ago. Why would Miss Stacy visit?

"I haven't done anything to disappoint you, have I?" she asked.

"It's nothing like that," Marilla replied. "She wanted to talk to you about going to college.

She thinks you're smart enough and wants you to take the exams."

"Really, Marilla?" Anne exclaimed. "Could it be true?"

"Of course, Anne," Marilla said. "Several children are preparing for the test—Jane Andrews, Josie Pye, Gilbert Blythe."

"Oh," said Anne scornfully. "Does this mean I'll have to study with Gilbert?" There was open rivalry between them ever since the day he had asked for her forgiveness—and she refused. He wouldn't even look at her. Anne was surprised at how much this bothered her. It didn't feel at all like winning. Deep down in her heart, she knew that if she could answer him again, she wouldn't say "no."

Their small study group met every day. Miss Stacy led them through Latin and math drills. By summer, everyone was tired from the hard work, but pleased with their progress.

Anne knew that this summer would be her last as a little girl. It wouldn't be long before she wore long skirts and put her hair up in a bun. So she meant to make the most of this summer and enjoy every last moment of it.

There was more talking than climbing trees, though. And more sitting and reading than acting out stories. She and Diana were happy just to spend this time together.

Diana wondered what would happen to them when they grew up. "I hope we can find someone rich to marry so we'll never have to worry."

"We are rich," said Anne. "Why, we have sixteen years to our credit, and we're happy as queens and we've all got imaginations, more or less. I'm quite content to be Anne of Green Gables."

Anne's last year at school passed quickly. She studied hard for the college entrance exam—and to beat Gilbert for the highest mark.

CHAPTER 19

The Pass List Is Out

Soon Anne and the study group were heading off to take the exam.

"Marilla, I just don't know what I'll do if I fail," said Anne.

"Why, you'll go back to school and try again next year," Marilla replied.

"I don't think I'd have the heart for it. If Gil—I mean, if the others passed and I didn't, it would crush me."

Before Anne set off to take the exam, Matthew declared that he knew she would beat the entire island. "You'll have the highest score. I just know it," he said.

It was a wonderful feeling to have someone with that much faith in her, but Anne worried about disappointing him.

"That will never happen," Matthew said with so much pride that Anne started to blush.

What Anne didn't know—because Marilla didn't tell her—was that Matthew wasn't feeling very well. His heart was bothering him. Even though Jerry Boot still helped him on the farm, he was tired out.

The exams were very hard and took several days. She and Gilbert often passed each other in the hall, but didn't say "hello." Anne wished she had accepted his offer of friendship. It would have been nice to have him to talk to.

They all returned to Avonlea. It would take three long, miserable weeks for the test scores to come out.

One day, Diana ran over to Green Gables with a newspaper in hand. "Anne," she called. "Anne! You've passed! And not just passed—you've come in first—you and Gilbert—it's a tie!"

Anne hugged her best friend in the whole world. She took the paper and ran to show Matthew.

CHAPTER 20

A Queen's Girl

The time came for Anne to leave for college. Both Anne and Marilla were reduced to tears—even Matthew's eyes were a little wet as they drove to the station. There was much hugging and promise of letters before Anne boarded the train.

Anne and her Avonlea friends—and Gilbert—registered at the Academy, then settled into their rooms. Since she and Gilbert had the top exam score, they were allowed to take extra classes. This meant they could get their teaching degree sooner. There was a lot of work ahead, but Anne knew their rivalry would spur them on.

Anne felt a bit lonely. She missed Green Gables and Diana, but was determined to work hard to earn the Gold Medal for highest marks. There was also the Avery Scholarship to think about. If she was lucky enough to receive it, she could spend another year at college.

Anne's homesickness wore off as she made new friends and threw herself into her work.

Although she and Gilbert took all the same classes, they still didn't speak. They kept up their race for top marks and just watched each other from afar. One thing that Anne did notice—and it bothered her more than she liked—was that Gilbert walked Ruby Gillis home from school every day.

It was hard to imagine them having much to say to each other. Ruby had even told Jane she didn't understand half of what Gilbert said. He talked just like Anne and always had his head in his books.

Anne didn't spend much time thinking about boys. Although she did think that if she and Gilbert were friends, they could walk home from the station together and have so much to talk about.

On the day final marks were announced, Anne and Jane walked into the main hall to learn who would receive the Gold Medal and the Avery Scholarship.

The hall was crowded. The first thing Anne saw was a group of boys carrying Gilbert on their shoulders—calling his name and cheering.

Anne's heart fell. So, she had lost after all. It would be hard to tell Matthew.

Suddenly, the students were calling out her name as well. "Three cheers for Anne Shirley—the winner of the Avery!"

"Oh, Anne," Jane said, "isn't it wonderful?"

For the first time in her life, Anne was speechless. It seemed that Gilbert had won the Gold Medal and she'd won the Avery. Her eyes filled with tears of joy.

CHAPTER 21

A Return to Avonlea

෴

Marilla and Matthew traveled to Charlottetown to see Anne graduate. They sat and watched her receive her diploma.

"Well," whispered Matthew, "aren't you glad we kept her after all?"

"It's not the first time I've been glad, Matthew Cuthbert," Marilla snorted. "And I'm sure it won't be the last."

Anne returned home with Marilla and Matthew. She thought Green Gables had never looked more beautiful. The first thing she did was run down to see Diana. It didn't take long before they were talking and laughing just like before.

"Does winning the Avery mean you won't be teaching next year?" Diana asked. They walked through the orchard as twilight settled.

"That's right," Anne replied. "I'll be going to Redmond College to study English. And the scholarship will pay all my expenses so Matthew and Marilla won't have to worry. Isn't that wonderful?"

"Oh, it is, Anne. Did you hear that the school in Newbridge offered Jane a job? And Gilbert will be teaching at the Avonlea school."

"Gilbert?" Anne was surprised. "But I thought he would go on to Redmond, as well."

"His father can't afford it," Diana said. "Gilbert is planning to earn his own way so he must start teaching right away."

Anne felt strange when she heard this news.

"It will be odd to go to school without Gil. It won't be the same."

The next morning at breakfast, Anne noticed that Matthew looked unwell. Marilla admitted that her brother was feeling poorly.

"His heart is troubling him," Marilla said. "He's been very tired lately."

"And how are you, Marilla?" Anne asked. "You're looking a little tired yourself. You shouldn't work so hard."

"It's not that, Anne," Marilla sighed. "It's my eyes. They're giving me terrible headaches. The doctor will be sending me to a specialist."

Sometimes Anne forgot that Matthew and Marilla were much older. And they worried about their savings, and the ailing Abbey Bank that held all their money. Anne began to worry.

Gently, Anne asked Marilla, "Have you heard anything new about the Abbey Bank?"

"Rachel has heard rumors that the bank isn't doing well," she replied. "I wanted Matthew to put our money in the Savings Bank in the first place, but old Mr. Abbey was such a good friend of Father and he'd always banked with him."

"Mr. Abbey is a very old man," Anne said. "Although he still holds the title of bank president, it is his nephews who have been running the institution."

She went out to the barn to talk to Matthew. "You've been working too hard today, Matthew. Why don't you take things easier?"

"It's only that I'm getting old, Anne, and keep forgetting it."

"If I had been the boy you sent for," said Anne, "I'd be able to spare you now in a hundred ways."

"Well, I'd rather have you than a dozen boys, Anne," said Matthew, patting her hand. "I guess it wasn't a boy that took the Avery Scholarship, was it? It was a girl—my girl—that I'm proud of."

Anne did her best to remember every moment of that night. It was the last night of her life before it was touched by sorrow. No life is ever quite the same after that.

CHAPTER 22

The Reaper Whose Name Is Death

❧

"Matthew—Matthew—what's the matter? Are you sick?"

It was Marilla who spoke, alarm in every word. Anne ran in from the hall, her hands full of flowers, in time to see Matthew fall to his knees by the front door. He held a piece of paper in his hand, his face drawn and gray. They rushed to him but were too late. He fell to the ground before they reached him.

"He's fainted," Marilla said. "Anne, run and tell Jerry Boot to get the doctor."

Jerry rushed off, telling Mrs. Lynde along the way. She hurried to Green Gables at once. As soon as Mrs. Lynde arrived, she took Matthew's pulse and put her ear to his chest. Tears came to her eyes.

"Oh, Marilla," she said gravely. "I don't think we can do anything for him."

"Mrs. Lynde, you don't think—you can't think Matthew is—is—" Anne dared not say that dreadful word.

"Yes, child, I'm afraid so. Matthew has died." Mrs. Lynde held on to Anne and Marilla's hands until the doctor arrived.

Dr. Blythe looked at Matthew, then at the paper he was holding. It was a letter from the Abbey Bank saying they had lost all of Matthew's money. This was the shock that proved too much for his weak heart.

Matthew's death proved a great shock for

Marilla. She cried so uncontrollably that people were amazed.

Anne, on the other hand, barely shed a tear. She was lost in thoughts of poor, sweet Matthew. It seemed too much to be without him. It wasn't until she was alone in bed—when she heard Matthew's voice saying, "My girl—my girl that I'm proud of"—that the tears came.

Marilla, hearing her sobs, came into her room to comfort her. They sat together holding one another through the night.

CHAPTER 23

Marilla Remembers

∽

A week after the funeral, Anne and Marilla sat on the front porch, watching the sunset.

"I guess Jane and Ruby are going to start teaching," Marilla said absentmindedly.

"Yes," Anne replied.

"And Gilbert Blythe? He's teaching this year, isn't he?"

"Yes." Anne's reply was very brief.

"What a nice-looking fellow he is," Marilla added. "I saw him at church last week and thought how much he looks like his father. John

Blythe was a nice boy. We used to be good friends, he and I. People called him my beau."

Anne looked up with interest. "Oh, Marilla, what happened? Why didn't you—?"

"We had a quarrel. I wouldn't forgive him. I was sulky and wanted to punish him. He never came back—the Blythes were all mighty independent. But I always kind of wished I'd forgiven him when I had the chance."

"So, you've had a bit of romance in your life, too," said Anne softly.

"Yes, I suppose so. You wouldn't think it to look at me. But you never can tell about people from their outsides. I'd forgotten all about it, until I saw Gilbert last Sunday."

CHAPTER 24

The Bend in the Road

cᴏ

Marilla kept her appointment with the eye doctor. She told Anne, "He says that if I give up all reading and sewing and wear these new glasses, my headaches should go away. But if not, there's a chance I will go blind."

Anne gasped. "Don't give up, Marilla. The doctor thinks you might be cured."

"But what am I to do, Anne, if I can't read or sew?" Marilla put on a brave face. "Never mind that now, child. Why don't you make me a cup of tea? I'm sure that will make me feel better."

A few days later, Anne saw Marilla talking with John Sadler. When Marilla came back into the kitchen, she told Anne, "He heard I was going to sell Green Gables and wants to buy it."

"Buy it! Buy Green Gables?" Anne wondered if she had heard right. "Oh, Marilla, no!"

"Anne, I don't know what else to do. I've thought this through. You are leaving and I can't run this place by myself."

"But you won't be alone, Marilla. I'm not going to Redmond," Anne cried.

"Not going to Redmond?! Whatever do you mean?"

"I'm not going to take the scholarship. You can't really believe I'd leave you here alone." Anne knelt beside Marilla's chair. "I have a plan.

"Mr. Barry wants to rent the farm for next year. I can't take the job at the Avonlea school because it's been promised to Gilbert. But I've applied for work over at the Carmody school. It's a bit far away, but we'll manage."

Marilla listened, astonished. "But Anne, you can't give up college. That's too much!"

"After you took me in and raised me?" Anne asked. "Nothing is too much for you, Marilla."

"But your studies?"

"Oh, I won't give them up. I can study at home and take courses by mail." Anne was starting to cheer up. "I have dozens of plans. You won't be able to keep up with them all."

"Well, I'm used to that," Marilla laughed.

When the rest of Avonlea heard the latest from Green Gables, there was much talk. As soon as Gilbert heard, he made some plans of his own. Mrs. Lynde was the one to reveal them to Anne.

"You won't be going to Carmody this fall, Anne-girl," Mrs. Lynde said. "It seems Gilbert Blythe asked the Avonlea trustees to take you,

ANNE OF GREEN GABLES

instead. So you won't have to travel back and forth. He'll teach at White Sands and board at the hotel. That's awful generous of him. Everyone knows he's saving for college."

"Oh, no," Anne whispered. "Gilbert shouldn't do that. That's too kind." Her eyes began to water.

The next day, Anne took a stroll through the orchard and around the Lake of Shining Waters. She noticed a tall boy walking toward her, whistling.

It was Gilbert. As soon as he saw Anne, he stopped whistling and turned his head. He started to pass without a hello.

"Gilbert," she said. Her cheeks began to blush. "I wanted to thank you for giving up the school for me. It was very good of you." She held out her hand to him.

He took the offered hand eagerly. "I was glad to do a small service. Are we to be friends

after this? Have you really forgiven me?"

Anne laughed and tried to withdraw her hand.

"I forgave you the day you rescued me from the water but have been too proud to admit it."

"We will be the best of friends," Gilbert said happily. "We were born to be friends. You've avoided destiny for far too long. So, come along, I'll walk you home."

Marilla looked curiously at Anne when she entered the kitchen.

"Who was it that walked you up the lane, Anne?"

"Gilbert Blythe," Anne said, realizing she was still blushing.

"I didn't think you were such good friends that you'd stand for half an hour by the gate talking," said Marilla with a dry smile.

"Were we really there that long? It seemed

just a few minutes. But, you see, we have five years to catch up on, Marilla."

Anne looked out the kitchen window. Life had found another bend in the road for Anne Shirley. She wondered what she would find next.

Questions, Questions, Questions
by Arthur Pober, Ed.D.

ভ

Have you ever been around a toddler who keeps asking the question "Why?" Does your teacher call on you in class with questions from your homework? Do your parents ask you questions at the dinner table about your day? We are always surrounded by questions that need a specific response. But is it possible to have a question with no right answer?

The following questions are about the book you just read. But this is not a quiz! They are designed to help you look at the people, places, and events in the story from different angles. These questions do not have specific answers. Instead, they might make you think of the story in a completely new way.

Think carefully about each question, and enjoy discovering more about this classic story.

1. How would you feel if you were Anne arriving at a new town and meeting a new family for the first time?

2. Mrs. Lynde thought Marilla and Matthew were taking a big risk in adopting a child. What was the biggest risk you've ever taken? When is taking risks important?

3. Anne believes that her red hair is different and ugly. Is that what we would believe today? What part of your appearance do you like best?

4. Anne likes to give new names to things. For instance, she calls a small road "the White Way of

Delight." Why do you think she does this? Have you ever made up names for things? Try renaming something near your house or school.

5. When Anne is told about meeting a new friend, she feels such excitement that she is afraid that she will be disappointed. Do you remember when you met your best friend? How did you feel? Did you know right away you would be friends?

6. Anne is full of nervous excitement when she arrives at her new school. What is the most excited you have ever felt?

7. Anne's green hair leads to all sorts of problems. Have you ever tried to make changes in your appearance that led to disastrous results? Why do you think Anne tried to dye her hair?

8. Both Diana and Anne think about what their lives will be like once they leave school. What do you think your life will be like in five, ten, or fifteen years?

9. Anne is an optimist. She always sees the positive side of things. Do you think you are an optimist?

10. What three words would you use to describe Anne? What three words would you use to describe yourself? How are you and Anne alike? How are you different?

Afterword

⌀

First impressions are important.

Whether we are meeting new people, going to new places, or picking up a book unknown to us, first impressions count for a lot. They can lead to warm, lasting memories or can make us shy away from any future encounters.

Can you recall your own first impressions and earliest memories of reading the classics?

Do you remember wading through pages and pages of text to prepare for an exam? Or were you the child who hid under the blanket to read with a flashlight, joining forces with Robin Hood to save Maid Marian? Do you remember only how long it took you to read a lengthy novel such as *Little Women*? Or did you become best friends with the March sisters?

Even for a gifted young reader, getting through long chapters with dense language can easily become overwhelming and can obscure the richness of the story and its characters. Reading an abridged, newly crafted version of a classic novel can be the gentle introduction a child needs to explore the characters and story line without the frustration of difficult vocabulary and complex themes.

Reading an abridged version of a classic novel gives the young reader a sense of independence and the satisfaction of finishing a "grown-up" book. And when a child is engaged with and inspired by a classic story, the tone is set for further exploration of the story's themes, characters, history, and details. As a child's reading skills advance, the desire to tackle the original, unabridged version of the story will naturally emerge.

If made accessible to young readers, these stories can become invaluable tools for understanding themselves in the context of their families and social environments. This is why the Classic Starts series includes questions that stimulate discussion regarding the impact and social relevance of the characters and stories today. These questions can foster lively conversations between children and their parents or teachers. When we look at the issues, values, and standards of past times in terms of how we live now, we can appreciate literature's classic tales in a very personal and engaging way.

Share your love of reading the classics with a young child, and introduce an imaginary world real enough to last a lifetime.

DR. ARTHUR POBER, ED.D.

Dr. Arthur Pober has spent more than twenty years in the fields of early-childhood and gifted education. He is the former principal of one of the world's oldest laboratory schools for gifted youngsters, Hunter College Elementary School, and former director of Magnet Schools for the Gifted and Talented for more than 25,000 youngsters in New York City.

Dr. Pober is a recognized authority in the areas of media and child protection and is currently the U.S. representative to the European Institute for the Media and European Advertising Standards Alliance.

THE STORM BOOK

The Storm

Story by Charlotte Zolotow

HarperTrophy
A Division of HarperCollins*Publishers*

Book

Pictures by Margaret Bloy Graham

To

Dr. Eugene Eisner,

who knows the child in

each of us

IT IS a day in the country, and everything is hot. The grass looks dry and parched. The buttercups are sticky with dust; the daisies' white petals look gray; and all the flowers, the rambler roses climbing up the gate, the hollyhocks leaning against the house, hang limply on their stems.

The little boy can almost see the heat quivering up like mist from the earth. A little caterpillar climbs carefully up a dusty blade of grass and then climbs down again. There is a special hot stillness over everything. The white fox terrier has crawled under the latticework of the porch and lies sleeping in the shade. Even the birds seem too hot to sing, for there is not a sound among the leaves.

But the hazy sky begins to shift, and the yellow heat turns gray. Everything is the same color—one enormous listless gray world where not a breath stirs and the birds don't sing. There isn't the slightest motion of a branch, the slightest whisper of a breeze. And still there is something expectant in the growing darkness; something is astir, something soundless and still for which the little boy waits.

He waits and he sees dark clouds beginning to form, throwing their shadow over the parched fields, moving one after another until they cover the sky and the world is black as night. A little cool wind suddenly races through the trees, sways the rambler roses, bends the daisies and buttercups and Queen Anne's lace and the long grass until they make a great silver sighing stretch down the hill.

Then it happens! Shooting through the sky like a streak of starlight comes a flash so beautiful, so fast, that the little boy barely has time to see the flowers straining into the storm wind.

"Oh, Mother," he calls, "*what was that?*"

"Lightning," his mother answers, "that our own lamplight comes from." The little boy thinks of the lamp in his room, with its warm golden glow. And he thinks of the lightning flashing through the sky. The lightning was like a wild white wolf running free in the woods and the lamp like the gentle white terrier who came when the little boy called.

And now from somewhere beyond the hill comes the great rolling rrrrrrrrrrrmmmmmmmmmmmmmmmmmDDDDDDDDDDDDDDDRRRR R R R R of the thunder.

"What's that?" the little boy shouts.

"Rain clouds breaking against each other, and that is the sound they make," his mother says. Now there is a silence again in the dark world, stillness, and then the whole sky lights up in one blinding starry flash of lightning.

The sky darkens again as the thunder draws closer, rolling loudly nearer, until, with a sudden explosion, it crashes overhead and a silver torrent of rain slants down. The daisies bend almost to the ground under the tearing weight of the wind and the rain sweeping over the rambler roses and trees, as they toss in the cool huge arms of the storm.

Miles away in the storm-darkened city, a young man closes his book and gets up to look out of the window. Below him on the street, the lighted store windows shine on the wet sidewalks and every flash of lightning shows people running by, newspapers over their heads or umbrellas held down in front of them to buffet the wind and the rain.

The tops of the tall buildings look cut off by the storm darkness, and the little city trees strain at their roots in their loop-fenced circles, and the wind whips the leaves from their branches. The automobile tires make a swish-swishing sound as they pass.

At the seashore an old fisherman stands boot-deep in the waves, and the wind and rain splatter against his oilskin with a terrible beating sound. His face is wet with sea spray and rain. When the thunder roars, nothing else can be heard, not the wild splashing of the black waves, nor the drive of the rain against the oilskin. It seems as though there is nothing in the world but the tremendous ear-splitting rrrrrMMM-MMMMDDDDDDDRRRRRRR R R R of the thunder, followed by streak after streak of cloud-rending light.

Once when the lightning flashes a little brown sandpiper skids across the sand on his way home, so swiftly that he is gone before the light leaves the sky.

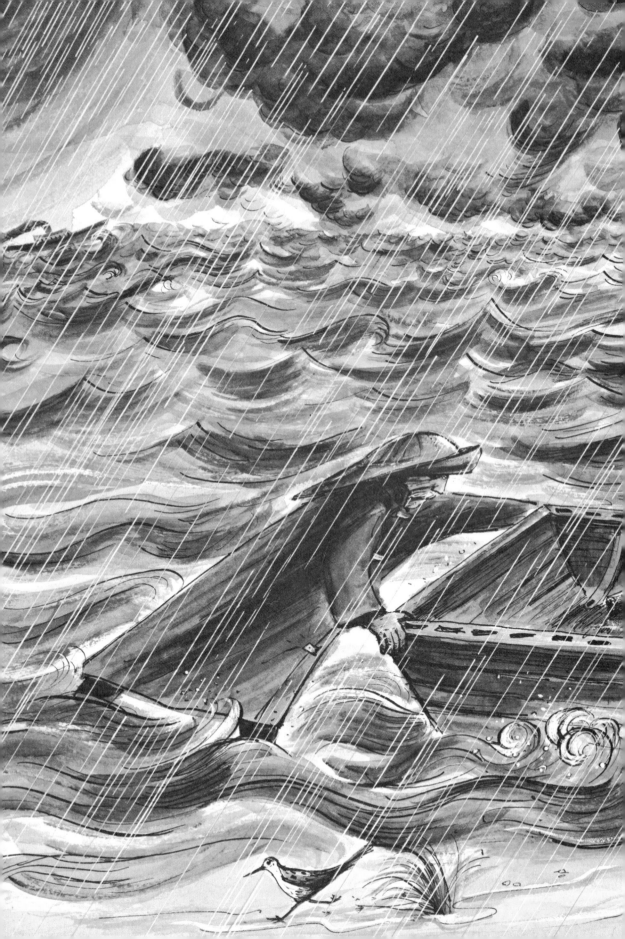

In the mountains the rain comes down like a waterfall. Each crash of thunder sounds as though the rocks of the mountains were splitting apart, but each flash of lightning shows them solid and quiet against the sky.

A young husband herds his sheep to shelter. His wife looks out of the window at the storm-torn hills, while their baby sleeps quietly in her arms.

The rain drives against the windows of the little boy's house. It beats a loud tattooing pitpatpitpatting on the roof, and the wind rising and falling in the trees sounds like the sea breaking against the shore.

Slowly the storm subsides. The sky begins to brighten, the thunder rolls away, and only from far, far off now can the little boy hear the rrrrrmmmmm-ddddrrrrr, as the wind blows the great clouds away from the cool wet land. The loud pitpatpitting on the roof grows softer, and softer, and slowly becomes a dull pit-a-pat, pit-pit-pit, and at last stops altogether. The air is clean and fresh, and smells of wet earth and growing things.

The rambler roses have covered the ground with a shower of wind-driven sweet-smelling petals. The daisies are still bent from the weight of the rain, and their moist white petals cling together. But already the buttercups are standing straight, fresh and glistening, with one clear raindrop cupped in each shiny yellow blossom.

A queer yellow light spreads over the earth now, so faint, so fine, so beautiful that the little boy lets out his breath with a soft whistling sound. And suddenly all the birds break into song. The glistening wet trees are loud with sharp quick twitterings and long full-noted calls.

Here and there in the sparkling grass a quick brown sparrow pecks around looking for worms. The light covers everything now, the house, the hollyhocks, the great stretch of grass, the trees, and the fresh cool face of the little boy who stands in the doorway watching.

"What's *that!*" he suddenly calls to his mother. She comes to the door and looks through the yellow light to a great curving misty arch of color that, coming from farther than they can see, bends across the sky, over the city; over the yellow storm-whipped sand; over the clean-smelling, bird-singing mountains; over the hill toward the little boy's door.

"That's the rainbow, little son," says his mother, "to show the storm has passed."

And she slipped her arm around him so gently he didn't notice, as he watched the beautiful sunlit colors arching over the world.